Little Red Riding Hood

ILLUSTRATED BY URBANTOONS

KING KI'EL

Once upon a time, inside the beautiful land of Kenya, lived a tribe known as the Maasai Warriors. These warriors sang and danced after every hunt, and the wild animals greatly feared them.

Leading the Maasai people was their noble King Mapinduzi, who everyone in the tribe respected and loved.

He married a beautiful woman, and she gave birth to an even more beautiful girl named Kiserian, which means 'the lucky one.' Kiserian lived with her father, King Mapinduzi, and her mother, Queen Umi, in a Kenyan village.

At the farthest end of the village was another lovely hut, where her grandmother lived.

Her grandmother once gave her a Maasai red cloak with a hood, which she always wore, so people called her Little Red Riding Hood.

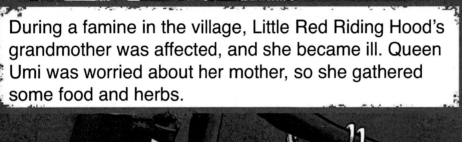

During a famine in the village, Little Red Riding Hood's grandmother was affected, and she became ill. Queen Umi was worried about her mother, so she gathered some food and herbs.

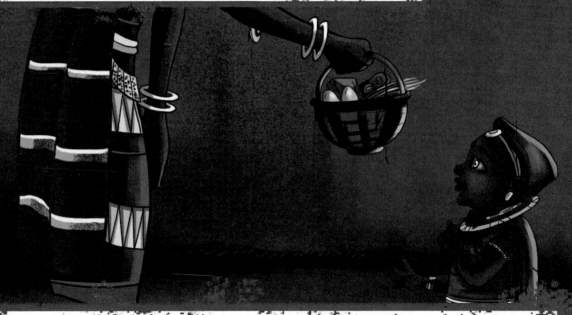

Her mother saw her unhappy face and whispered in her ear, "Don't worry, my darling daughter, just give her the medicine and food, and she will be just fine." She then called Little Red Riding Hood and said, "Put on your hood, you must go to see your grandmother. Take along this basket for her."

It was a bright and sunny African morning. All around, Little Red Riding Hood grew the beautiful wild Kenyan flowers that she loved so well, and she stopped to pick a bunch for her grandmother.

After some time, she reached her destination. The flowers were glittery in the bright sunlight, and their aromas filled the air.

She stopped to pick a flower when, from behind her, a gruff voice said, "Asubuhi njema, good morning, Little Red Riding Hood." Little Red Riding Hood turned around and saw a great big black panther. But she was not afraid, as she did not know what a wicked beast the panther was.

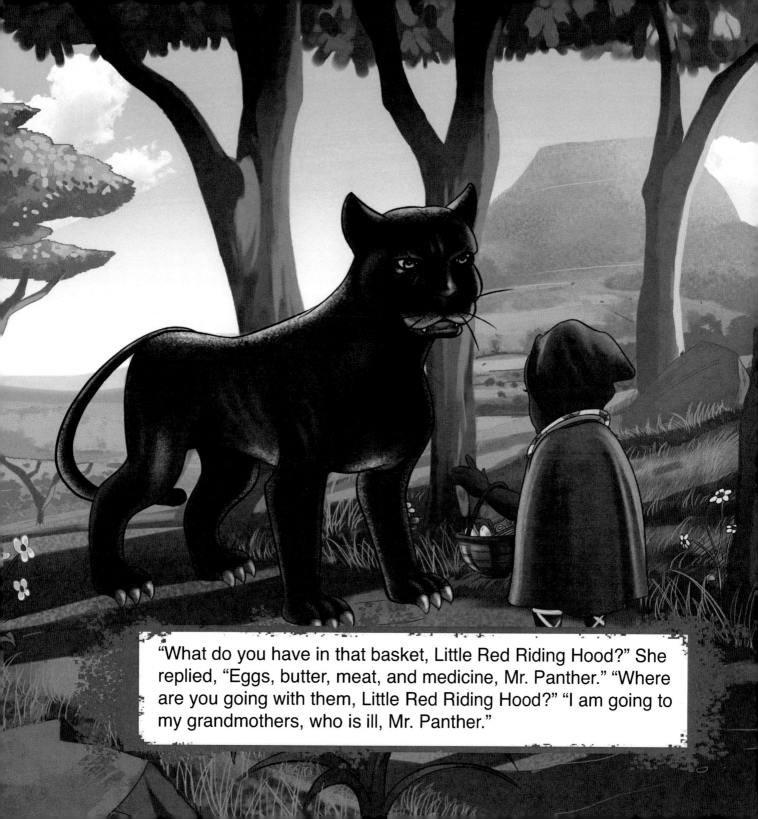

"What do you have in that basket, Little Red Riding Hood?" She replied, "Eggs, butter, meat, and medicine, Mr. Panther." "Where are you going with them, Little Red Riding Hood?" "I am going to my grandmothers, who is ill, Mr. Panther."

"Where does your grandmother live, Little Red Riding Hood?"
"Along that path, past the wild rose bushes, then through the gate at the end of the woods, Mr. Panther."

Mr. Panther then said again, "Asubuhi njema, good morning," and set off. Little Red Riding Hood continued her search for wildflowers.

At last, he reached grandmother's hut and knocked at the door. "Who is there?" called grandmother. "Little Red Riding Hood," answered the wicked panther in his softest voice. "Open the door and come in!" replied grandmother.

He made one leap at grandmother, but she jumped out of bed into a closet. Then the panther put on the cap which she dropped and crept under the covers.

Shortly after, Little Red Riding Hood knocked at the door and walked in, saying, "Good morning grandmother, I have brought you eggs, butter, meat, and medicine, and a bunch of flowers I gathered in the woods."

"All the better to eat you up with, my dear," The panther yelled as he dived at Little Red Riding Hood.

At the same time, the King and his warriors were returning from their hunting trip. They were very happy, singing and dancing along the way.

But during their return to the village, they passed the Queen's mother's hut and heard a scream.

They rushed in, and the King saw the panther attacking his beautiful daughter. Angry and eager to save her, the King attacked the panther with his spear and threw it at the panther, pinning him against the wall.

The King and his soldiers then tied the panther up by its hands and feet. They carried him out of the hut and locked the panther up to stop him from harming anyone else.

Little Red Riding Hood's father carried her home, and everyone was happy that she had escaped the panther.

Little Red Riding Hood and her father sat down after they returned to the hut. He told her that every stranger wasn't her friend, and to be more careful.

The Maasai Warrior hugged his daughter and told her he loved her very much.

The King and his sons taught Little Red Riding Hood Maasai spear throwing and Maasai karate, so she could defend herself if she ever needed to again, and they all lived happily ever after.
THE END

PANTHER PRIDE

READING AGE
6 TO 9

In the Land of ancient China, a group of black panthers lived in harmony together, until the humans took their land for new buildings. Frustrated and angry, the Panthers gathered all of the animals to start an animal revolution and take their land back. Will the animals win? Great book for boys and girls.

$9.99

ISABELLA

READING AGE 8 - 15

Beautiful, smart, and kind, Isabella lived a charmed life in Puerto Rico until her beloved mother died. Her father remarried, bringing two selfish "sisters" into Isabella's home. Now Isabella is Cinderella, pretty much a servant to her stepsisters. When the prince is looking for a wife, will Cinderella's natural beauty shine through?

$12.99

I LOVE MY NATURAL CROWN
(NURSERY RHYMES)

READING AGE
4 TO 6

Urbantoonsreleases, Dashikee Kids, "I love my Natural Crown," a book of nursery rhymes for young girls that teaches self-love, confidence and embracing the beauty of natural hair.

$7.99

THE ADVENTURES OF
JAHLONI & JAHBRIL

READING AGE
6 TO 15

Urbantoons The Adventures of Jahloni & Jahbril is about two Rastafarian boys who finds a magical ancient book hidden under their parents bed. Once opened, it turns them into superheros and sends them into another universe filled with Dinosaurs and new adventures.

$11.99

VITILIGO BEAUTY

READING AGE
6 TO 15

Urbantoons' Vitiligo Beauty is a great children's book for young girls with the skin condition Vitiligo. Vitiligo beauty is a retelling of the story of Snow White. This book is great self-esteem booster, with a rich story. It's a must-have book for your young girl.!

$9.99

LITTLE RED RIDING HOOD

READING AGE 8 - 15

In this classical updated children's story taken place in the beautiful land of Africa. Little Red Riding Hood is slightly cautious when her grandmother looks suspiciously like a sly Panther. Children of all colors will eagerly continue reading to see what will happen when the Panther shows how big and sharp his teeth are!

$9.99

PETER PAN

READING AGE
6 TO 9

A new twist on the classic Peter Pan fairy tale. In this version of the story, Peter is especially concerned about the fate of two African slave children. When Tinker Bell becomes jealous of one of the children, everyone's fate is at stake.

$9.99

CINDERELLA

READING AGE
6 TO 15

Beautiful, smart, and kind, Safiya lived a charmed life in Italy until her beloved mother died. Her father remarried, bringing two selfish "sisters" into Safiya's home. Now Safiya is Cinderella, pretty much a servant to her stepsisters. When the prince is looking for a wife, will Cinderella's natural beauty shine through?

$9.99

PINOCCHIO

READING AGE
6 TO 15

The story of America's favorite puppet is now being told in the city of brotherly love. Sonny is an older and wiser puppet maker from Philadelphia who only had one wish in life. Now Pinocchio is alive and Sonny's trying to keep him safe and on the right path in these Philly streets.

$14.99

MANSA MUSA

READING AGE
8 - 15

Urbantoons "Mansa Musa", is a story about the rise of a young African boy named Musa, who grew up humbly in the Mali Empire under the King Sundiata. Groomed to a royal guard for the king. Musa had a bigger dream. His dream was bigger and he lived to be the richest king to ever live.

$14.99

I WILL BE GREAT

READING AGE
5 TO 10

Urbantoons releases, King of Mali, "I WILL BE GREAT!" is a book of nursery rhymes mixed with positive affirmations for young boys.

$7.99

MY DADDY DOES
MY HAIR

READING AGE
6 TO 9

This book was written to tell the story of all the fathers who will go to the moon and back for their daughters. It's the first day of school, and dad needs help on how to style his daughter's hair, so what does he do?

$9.99

BLACK HISTORY PUZZLE

Marcus Garvey — 42 PIECES

Michelle Obama — 42 PIECES

President Barack Obama — 42 PIECES

URBANTOONSINC.COM

URBANTOONS BOOK BUNDLES

KING OF MALI
PINOCCHIO
PETER PAN
PANTHER PRIDE
JAHLONI AND JAHBRIL

SNOW WHITE
LITTLE RED RIDING HOOD
ISABELLA
I LOVE MY NATURAL CROWN
CINDERELLA

URBANTOONSINC.COM

URBANTOONS COLORING BOOK COLLECTION

Mansa Musa Coloring Book $8.99

Melanin Beauty Coloring Book $8.99

Cinderella Coloring Book $8.99

Peter Pan Coloring Book $8.99

Pinocchio Coloring Book $8.99

I Love my Natural Coloring Book $7.99

URBANTOONSINC.COM

Made in the USA
Coppell, TX
24 August 2022

81947204R00019